STORMING HIS HEART

NICOLE BLANCHARD

DEDICATION

*For my all the girlies who are as obsessed
with the secret baby trope as I am*

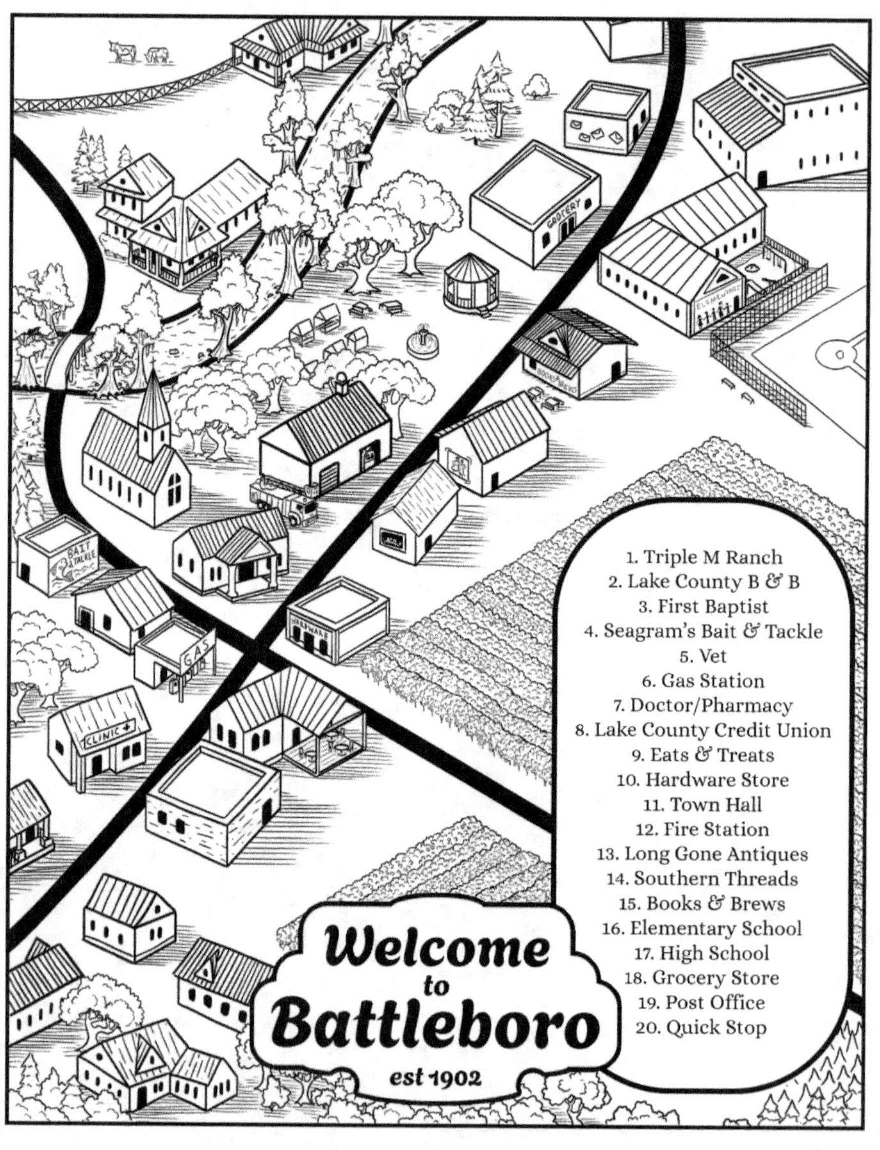

GROCERY
ELEMENTARY
BOOKS & BREWS
BAIT & TACKLE
HARDWARE
GAS
CLINIC +
1. Triple M Ranch
2. Lake County B & B
3. First Baptist
4. Seagram's Bait & Tackle
5. Vet
6. Gas Station
7. Doctor/Pharmacy
8. Lake County Credit Union
9. Eats & Treats
10. Hardware Store
11. Town Hall
12. Fire Station
13. Long Gone Antiques
14. Southern Threads
15. Books & Brews
16. Elementary School
17. High School
18. Grocery Store
19. Post Office
20. Quick Stop
Welcome to Battleboro
est 1902

CONTENTS

1. Avery   1
2. Avery   11
3. Walker   19
4. Avery   25
5. Walker   31
6. Avery   39
7. Walker   45
8. Avery   53
9. Walker   61
10. Avery   67
11. Walker   75
12. Avery   81
Epilogue   89

Acknowledgments   93
About Nicole Blanchard   95
Also by Nicole Blanchard   97

CHAPTER 1
AVERY

A boom shakes the house and a whiplash of pure, primal fear invades the tiny spaces in my body. Sensing my unease, the little life in my arms lets out a disgruntled squeal as hot tears leak from her reddened, tired eyes—eyes a blue-gray, the same color of the stormy evening sky outside the window. Neither of us has gotten much sleep today. I expect we won't get any tonight either. As if to confirm my thoughts, lightning flashes, turning the living room from night to day in one quick instant.

"Shh, shh, it's okay. It's going to be okay. I promise. It's only a storm." I wasn't sure if she could hear me over the roaring wind and lashing of rain against the tin roof. "A really, really loud storm. We get them all the time."

This isn't *any* storm, but I can't tell her that. At a couple months old, my words are to soothe myself more than her.

All she knows is her mom is terrified. No doubt she can sense the sour tang of my fear coming off me in waves.

"That baby needs a bottle. Sounds like she's starvin'."

I close my eyes for a moment, then turn to my grandmother. She sits in her customary rocking chair, a green so worn it's nearly gray. "She's not hungry. She's just scared, is all."

Her and me both.

Grandma Rosie purses her lips and rocks more vigorously in her chair. I hold my baby closer and ignore her. Nearly eighty and suffering from dementia, Grandma Rosie has a habit of repeating herself and calling me by my mother's name. She also has a tendency for bluntness—which most people would classify as straight meanness—but I know that's the disease talking. Grandma Rosie raised me and before her brain started failing her, she'd been the sweetest woman alive.

That's why I bite my tongue and turn away from the living room, moving deeper into the house. The baby wails so loud it almost drowns out the wind and rain. Almost.

Readjusting her little body against my shoulder, I cradle her head and pat her back as I rock her back to a sense of calm. Soothing her helps me, albeit only slightly. Once she settles a little, I reach for my phone in my back pocket to check the weather again. I'm praying for a miracle with every atom of my being, though the only miracle I've ever witnessed is finally sleeping in my arms.

Please, please shift. Shift away from here.

I close my eyes as the weather radar loads and my heart thuds like a hammer in my chest. The last thing I want is to condemn someone else to the horror of what's to come, but at the selfish, human center of me, I'd rather it'd go somewhere else, anywhere else.

Please.

If I'd been stronger, I would have convinced Grandma Rosie to evacuate this morning. Dammit, I should have carried her out kicking and screaming if I had to, but she wouldn't budge.

"I've lived here for fifty years and I'll die here," had been her litany all day despite my pleading. I couldn't leave her to die all alone and confused. She didn't have anyone else but me.

So I'd spent the entire day battening down the hatches. I'd boarded up the windows, done last-minute runs for emergency supplies. Grandpa Jim had kept an old weather radio that still worked if only by the grace of God alone, so I'd have something in case the power and cell service went out.

Most people thought the hurricane would weaken as it came closer to the gulf. Most hurricanes that hit our area of Northern Florida did—in fact it's a running joke that most Floridians have hurricane parties to celebrate their landfall. But according to the radar and the Facebook Live from our local weatherman, Hurricane Michael hasn't weakened. It's grown stronger. It's predicted to make landfall as a Category 5. One of the strongest to ever hit our area.

And it's supposed to be heading right for us.

My phone wobbles in my hands as the weatherman's words ring in my ears. A Category 5. You hear about them, sure, and we've gotten some bad storms throughout the years, but

nothing like this. A storm like this could obliterate every-thing. We are far inland, thankfully, so we won't get the brunt of the storm surge or the worst of the winds. I try to take a seed of hope from that thought and immediately feel guilty. So many people on the coast like me haven't evacuated.

The baby lets out a mewl of protest and I realize I'm squeezing her too close. I let out a shuddering breath and move from the kitchen to the room we share. Carefully so as not to wake her, I tuck her into her bassinet while I finish last-minute preparations. Really, I'm not sure what else I can do to save us, but I have to try.

With every hour that passes, the storm moves inexorably closer. Despite my fervent prayers, or perhaps because God knows I've never prayed with any intention before, it doesn't shift away. All of the models predict it'll make landfall and move right over us.

"What the devil?" I hear Grandma Rosie shout sometime later. "My pictures done turned off."

Moving from the hall bathroom where I've been filling the tub with extra water and organizing our first aid supplies, go-bags of food and clothes for each of us, and Grandma Rosie's medical supplies, I join her in the living room. The ancient television she insists on keeping to watch local channels is filled with snow. The sight of the gray static sends a spear of fear straight into my gut.

I check my phone and note I still have service. "C'mon, I can put your shows on for you on my tablet, but we have to watch in the bathroom."

"In the bathroom?" she repeats, aghast. "What in the world for?"

"It's the only place it'll work in the storm," I improvise. "I'll call the cable company and see if I can get your regular shows fixed, but for now this will have to do."

She blusters and dillydallies, but I manage to get her to sit on the toilet while I roll the baby's bassinet inside with us.

Luckily, she's still sound asleep, so at least I don't have to worry about her still being afraid. Grandma Rosie is oblivious, so she won't be scared either. As I close the door behind us, I thank my lucky stars for that blessing because I'm scared enough for all three of us.

It lasts forever.

It's over in an instant.

I'm not certain which is true, maybe both.

Grandma Rosie isn't even hollering anymore. She sits on the toilet, rocking herself back and forth and carries on a conversation with Grandpa Jim like he's sitting right next to her. The baby woke up a while ago and after nursing, she contented herself with a pacifier and went back to sleep. I keep her in a sling wrap, close to my chest, because it's the safest place I can think to have her. I can't bear to let her out of my sight.

Unwelcome and unhelpful tears trail down my cheeks no matter how much I try to swipe them away. They're part fear, but mostly frustration. Everything I've worked so hard to achieve over the past two years could be ripped from my grasp—literally. This house is old. Grandma Rosie and Grandpa Jim bought it new when they were first married, but it's fallen into disrepair since his death. I don't even know if it'll withstand the 100-mile-an-hour winds. All of my possessions, all of the baby's things I'd painstakingly collected, and everything Grandma Rosie holds dear, could be sucked away in a moment. The thought fills me with a black, sucking despair.

The roaring sound intensifies. My hands are shaking too hard to manage my phone, so I don't try. My last radar check told me the eye of the storm was about to pass overhead, so another look would be pointless. The weather radio works in fits and spurts. Artificial light from the electric lantern washes everything in an eerie orange glow.

"Oh, Jim," I hear Grandma Rosie wail. The sound cuts me deep.

If I'm scared, I can't imagine what it must be like for her to be here, not really knowing where or even when she is with the madness going on around her.

"It's all right, Grandma Rosie," I say, even though I'm not certain she can hear me over the noise. "It's Avery. I'm right here with you. It's going to be okay."

"Where's Jim? I want Jim."

I dry my tears. Rosie and the baby need me to be strong for both of them. There's no use in crying. "We'll find him when the storm is over, Grandma, I promise. I'll be here with you until it's over. It can't be much longer now."

If the eye of the storm is close, that means we'll hit the other wall and then it'll go on to terrorize someone else. I cling to these thoughts as the winds beat at the walls, as some of the tin roof over our heads begins to peel away and slap against the slats underneath. *SLAP SLAP SLAP.* The sound is so loud I feel it in the backs of my teeth. The baby jumps against my chest and then settles again, snuggling closer. Thank goodness for small mercies. I kiss her head and murmur, "I love you," against her sweet-smelling skin.

Because I do, more than I ever thought I could, more than I've ever loved anything in this world. I'd make it through this for her, for them. I have to.

There's a boom and a large, shuddering crash from

outside. I jolt and hug the baby tighter to me, rocking when she frets a little. I'm afraid to imagine what the sound could have been. A branch falling. A car being thrown by a gust of wind. The last news reports I'd watched had been of two storm chasers nearly drowned in the storm surge in Mexico Beach. We're landlocked here, but with a storm this bad a car being thrown about wouldn't be outside the realm of possibilities.

You've seen too many movies, Avery-girl.

Great. Now I'm not the only one hearing Grandpa Jim.

All at once, the roaring sound stops and the quiet is almost as deafening for its absence. The runaway hammering of my heartbeat replaces the wind, and it takes me a moment to realize we must be in the eye. I'm equal parts relieved and terrified because it means we have the other wall to go through before this nightmare is over.

The only thought that keeps me from going completely insane is the thought that it'll be over. There will be an end. It may not seem like it now, but it can't last forever. No matter how much it seems like it.

Water drip, drip, dripping reaches my ears through the stillness. I have enough presence of mind to give a passing thought to the damage it could cause. Then I have to laugh at myself. We'll be lucky if we still have a roof over our heads when this is over, let alone a little water damage.

Soon, there's no time to think. The roaring wind returns, and it begins again. A hand reaches out for me and I look up to find Grandma Rosie solemn and lucid—which is so rare it distracts me for a moment from the horrors outside.

"Grandma Rosie?" I croak out.

"Don't worry. It'll be okay. Just a little rain." Her smile is tremulous, but warm and so like the woman who raised me that I manage to smile back, despite everything.

Her words are nearly identical to the ones I said only a few hours before—a sentiment I'll have to revisit when I have a spare moment to think on it more.

The baby in my hands lets out a little sound in her sleep and Grandma Rosie says, "What a sweet baby. What's her name?"

"Rosalynn Grace. I named her after you." I don't know why it seems so important to tell her this now, of all times, but I force the words out in a rush over the din.

"A mouthful for a little girl." Grandma Rosie's eyes begin to cloud over. "You should call her Gracie."

"I will," I say, but she's already gone, her eyes glued to the tablet where I've downloaded her favorite shows for her. It hasn't gone dead yet, but it must be on its last legs. I don't have a generator, so Lord only knows what I'll do when the last dregs of juice drain away. I doubt there will be power anywhere if we make it out of this.

I doubt there will be much of anything for a long, long time.

CHAPTER 2
AVERY

I settle Grandma Rosie into her bed, thankful she still has one. She has one bar of battery left on her tablet, but it should be enough to help her off to sleep. I leave the lantern in her room in case she wakes up in the middle of the night and tries to wander around, as she's prone to do. I'd done a thorough once-over of her room and found the only damage was a broken window from the porch swing I'd forgotten to take down.

It could have been worse.

So, so much worse.

A broken window, damaged roof, those were things I could come back from. The complete loss of the house, or someone I loved? There's no coming back from that.

I settle onto the couch in the living room after cleaning up the glass. One of the flashlights sits beside me, pointed up at the ceiling. It's a poor substitute for the lantern, but beggars can't be choosers. From what I can glean from the radio and the spotty cell reception I have, rescue efforts are underway, but it's an arduous, painstaking process. The sheer number of downed trees is incalculable, making it hard for rescue operations to commence.

Needless to say, there won't be anyone coming through tonight and I haven't even looked outside to see what shape my car is in. I'm afraid to. One catastrophe at a time is all I have the energy to face. I'll deal with figuring out our next steps and clearing away debris tomorrow.

Now that the adrenaline is fading, weariness settles over me. I arrange baby Rosie's bassinet next to the couch. While she nurses, I attempt to connect to the internet, but it's next to impossible and loads indefinitely. It's strange, being so disconnected. It's isolating and in a weird way freeing all at once.

It's then that I remember the battery pack I use to charge my phone on vacations—or when I used to take vacations. I'd plugged it in when I first realized the storm was coming and there was no way Grandma Rosie was leaving her house, meaning I'd be stuck here too unless I wanted to condemn her to a horrific fate. Once the baby is done nursing and is once again sound asleep—thank goodness—I tuck her into her bassinet and retrieve the battery pack and charger cord.

Thankfully, it has half a charge, which allows me to hook up both my phone and the tablet, which I retrieve from a snoring Grandma Rosie's room. I take a full water bottle on my way back to the couch and a granola bar to stave off the breastfeeding munchies that will inevitably come. Once I polish off the granola bar and half of the water, I finally— finally—allow myself to relax into the couch with the baby close beside me. Sleep finds me easier than I thought it would.

"I want eggs and bacon," Grandma Rosie announces way too damn early the next morning.

I blink blearily up at her hovering over me at the couch. "What—what?"

"Look at you sleeping the day away. It's morning time. Time to wake up." She shuffles over to her rocking chair, freshly charged tablet in hand. "Up, up, up. Everybody up. If I can't sleep, nobody sleeps."

"I'm up, I'm up." With a quick look at the baby, who is blissfully still asleep, I push to sitting.

The first thing I notice is the heat.

Then, I remember the night before.

The storm.

"I don't think we have power for eggs, but I can make you some cereal." I'd packed some of the contents of our fridge in a cooler while I was prepping the day before. The milk should still be good for a while.

Grandma Rosie harrumphs, but doesn't argue. Good. Maybe today will be a good day for her, relatively.

The front door protests when I try to open it, swollen from the moisture and humidity. When it opens, it's to an alien world on the other side. My hand flies to my mouth as I gasp. The front yard looks like a jungle. Several trees had toppled over. One thick oak limb lies horizontally across most of our fence, obscuring the front walk. Another has fallen over the front porch, its limbs spiderwebbing inside like a corpse's fingers. Dozens, hundreds, of smaller branches litter everything.

Debris covers the roads in front of the house along with more fallen limbs. I don't even see how we'd get help even if we needed it. There won't be any trucks on the roads until they can get them cleared and that'll take a couple men and a half dozen chainsaws. A water main has busted across the street, flooding a neighbor's yard. Several limbs crush another's car and my eyes fly to my own busted up sedan. Aside from debris blown on top, it's relatively, shockingly, unscathed—not that it'll do us any good now.

All we can do for the time being is sit still and stay out of the way. I don't know how long it'll take, but I do know there will be crews out at some point to help clear the roads, fix the downed power lines, and check on residents to make sure no one is injured. God, I hope no one has been injured.

Once I feed Grandma Rosie and the baby, I'll take a more thorough look outside, make sure there's no one close by who needs help. Then…I don't know. One step at a time, I suppose. That's all any of us can do.

While I'm making bowls of cereal, I attempt to check online for any news. The loading symbol at the top of my phone keeps going round and round and the pages stay blank. I don't know if all the towers are down or if it's taking a long time because of general chaos or what. It's strange not being connected to anything at all. It makes me feel very alone.

By the time we sit down at the small dinette table, it's nearly ten or so in the morning and already sweltering. It was a warm October before the storm, but it has to be in the high eighties, if not higher. Our house stays cool, but it won't for long if the temperature keeps rising. Once I find a way out of here and make sure no one is injured, my first priority will be to find a generator. Perhaps I can plug a window unit into it and keep our small living room cool, at least. The nights won't be so bad, but a hot Florida afternoon can be killer.

Later, I leave Grandma Rosie watching her shows and baby Gracie napping deeply. With the baby monitor receiver clipped to my belt, I strap on a pair of old sneakers and head outside for the first time since the storm. By the time I make it through the front yard to the gate, my legs are scraped to all hell and I realize all the fallen trees have disturbed dozens and dozens of yellow jacket nests. I'm stung twice and am left cursing and sweating, already lathered up in a mood.

Hissing through my teeth, I work my way across the road to my closest neighbor. I'm almost to their steps when I hear their shouts from the other side of the closed door.

"Hello? Can you hear us? We're trapped inside!"

I speed up picking through the debris on their porch—including a large downed limb that's wedged in their doorway, completely blocking the majority of their front windows and their front door. Quickening my pace, I shout back, "Mary? Tom? It's Avery. I'm coming!"

"Avery, thank God," comes Mary's relieved voice. "We've been hollering all morning. There's another limb that damn near crashed through the back door. We'd jump out the windows if I didn't fret about Tom breaking a hip."

"Fool woman," I hear Tom mutter, which makes me smile despite everything.

"You guys say there. I'm going to find a way to get inside."

The limb is the size of a small tree. There's no way I'll be able to move the damn thing, but I try nonetheless, to no avail. The windows on either side of the house are over my head, so there'll be no climbing up unless I can find something to stand on. They weren't kidding about the back being caved in. Half a rotten tree collapsed on it.

I come back around to the front, hoping I can wiggle my way in between the tree and the front door to get it open. Above the sound of distant buzzing chainsaws and humming yellow Tomets, I begin to hear the sound of more voices, some raised over the din. More people must be up and moving around trying to clear out paths, discern the extent of damage.

The crunch of boots on leaves snapping twigs has me looking up as I near Tom and Mary's front steps. Maybe it's someone who can help.

I open my mouth to call out to them when the words die on my tongue.

The man hasn't noticed me yet. He carries a chainsaw with one hand like it doesn't weigh a thing. He scans the area, sharp and observant. I know that gaze. I've stared into it, dreamed of it. His eyes haunt me every day.

"Walker," I say, louder than I intend, because it's the only thing I know about him other than what it feels like to have him inside me.

He stops. Turns to me.

Those blue-gray eyes meet mine.

CHAPTER 3
WALKER

PAST

"I don't normally do this," is all I remember her saying before she tugs me to my Airbnb.

"Neither do I."

She pushes open the door and stumbles inside. "No, I mean it. That's not just a line. I don't go home with strange guys."

When I'm over the threshold, she pushes it shut behind me and presses me against its surface. My brain short-circuits like it had the moment I saw her in the bar. Sounds cliché, but they're clichés for a reason.

She'd been waiting tables at the restaurant I'd gone to for dinner. Not my waitress, but one a couple sections over. I'd lingered over a mediocre steak and over-dry baked potato that I'd washed down with cheap beer to watch her like some kind of creep. I'd stayed through dinner rush, then wandered over to the bar where she'd taken over serving drinks. She plied me with alcohol until I, with some stroke of luck or fate or both, convinced her to go to the bar next door when we couldn't stay at the restaurant any longer. Some hours later, with enough alcohol to make bad decisions sound like good ones, I'd convinced her to come back to my place where we could be alone.

"I'm not complaining," I say and let my hands wander wherever she'll allow them. "I wouldn't judge you even if you did."

She pauses her own explanation to peer up at me with fathomless brown eyes. "That's so sweet," she says, causing me to laugh. "What did you say your name was again?"

"Walker," I answer and brush back her loose brown curls from her face. God, I want to kiss her.

"I'm Avery."

"I remember."

She presses her eyes shut, sighs a little. "We should probably talk some more. Get to know each other better. I think I'm a little drunk."

I close my eyes and lean my head against the door, praying for some self-control. "Whatever you want. I just don't want to be alone."

Her fingers pause their exploration of my chest over the thin material of my T-shirt. I glance back down at her, watching her study me. Fuck, maybe she was right. I'd had way too much to drink.

"I don't want to be alone either," she confesses.

Wanting nothing more than to taste those confessions on her lips, I instead put my hands on her arms and put some much-needed distance between us. "Why don't you sit down? I'll make us some coffee. I think there's some in the kitchen."

At this, she chuckles and carefully sits on the small

leather sofa in the living room. "You don't know if you have coffee in your own house?"

"It's not mine," I answer as I hunt through the cabinets searching for K-cups. "It's an Airbnb. I was only in town for a few months. Didn't seem like it would make much sense to rent a place for longer when I'd be leaving soon."

"Oh, so you aren't from Battleboro?" Was I imagining it or was there disappointment in her voice? I like the thought of her wanting to have me around. Not many people do these days.

"I am originally. Just back while I'm in between jobs." I find the K-cups, an off-brand, but they'll do, and load one up in the machine. While it gurgles to life, I lean against the countertop and grip its edge to keep my hands from reaching for her. "I'm a Wildland Firefighter."

She nods, then laughs. "I have no idea what that means."

"You know those big wildfires you hear of on the news out west?"

Avery's eyes widen. "You fight with those?"

"Nine months out of the year. I'm in between contracts right now, but I'm going back for another contract in a few days."

"So, what brings you back to Florida?" she asks. "Why not stay out west all year round?"

Good question. I consider my words while I make one cup and start another. "You want cream or sugar?" I ask.

"Both," she says.

I stir them in and finally answer, "Family, I guess."

She makes a noise of understanding in her throat as she sips her coffee. "That'll do it. That's why I've stayed here. I've never been out of the state. I imagine it's pretty different where you go, even without the firefighters."

"You'll have to go sometime. Nothing like it."

She takes the offered coffee cup and smiles sadly. "Thanks. Maybe one day."

"What about you? What do you do when you're not working at the restaurant or bartending?" I sit on the small recliner with my own cup of coffee and suck it back even though it's piping hot. I could use the mental clarity before I do something stupid. Like beg her to stay with me.

"Not much," Avery answers with a self-deprecating laugh. "I'd like to go back to school one day, but for now all I do is work. Nothing as exciting as fighting wildfires." She lets out a yawn, then an embarrassed laugh. "I'm sorry, it's been a long day. I worked a double shift. The coffee is sobering me up, but unfortunately, I'm still dog tired. Some company I am, huh?"

"Do you want to crash here?" I ask before I can stop myself. At her curious glance, I say, "Just sleep, I promise. Or I can call someone to take you home."

She's already shaking her head before I finish the suggestion. "No, that's okay. Um, if it's not weird, I can sleep here and walk back to my car in the morning. I mean, if you're okay with that."

Okay with it? It'd be a relief not to wake up all alone shrouded in nightmares. "I don't mind. As long as you don't care if I snore."

Avery giggles. "I'm so tired, I probably won't even notice."

"Let me get you some clothes." The skin-slick jeans and tight restaurant T-shirt don't leave anything to the imagination, but they also probably wouldn't be comfortable to sleep in. Plus, I like the thought of having her in my stuff, my scent on her skin. Like an indelible mark in some way.

"Thanks. I appreciate it."

I take her empty cup and my half-drunk mug to the sink and retrieve a loose T-shirt and a pair of sweatpants from my suitcase in the bedroom. When I turn, she's already standing at the door, watching me. I'd be lying if I said having her near me with a bed so close didn't make me think of her in it —without the clothes.

"I'll let you get changed."

While she undresses in the bedroom, I change into another pair of sweatpants in the attached bath. I do us both the courtesy of brushing my teeth and ignore the red-eyed reflection in the mirror. She's lying under the covers when I come out. Maybe I like seeing her there more than I should.

You're a lonely piece of shit, Walker.

But I get into bed with her anyway, sliding in between the sheets to soak up her warmth. Without any urging, she scoots to my side and wraps her arm around my waist like we'd been doing this for years. Maybe it hadn't been her looks that had stopped me from going home by myself. Maybe the lost parts in me had recognized something similar in her.

I mean to tell her I don't normally do this either, but for the first time in months, I fall asleep without wondering what nightmares are waiting for me.

CHAPTER 4
AVERY

Maybe I didn't make it through the storm.

Maybe this is all a dream.

I never thought I'd see him again after that night, though I'd done enough social media stalking to try and find him. Kind of hard to do when I didn't even know his last name.

Walker doesn't break stride, merely shifts his destination to my direction, his long, lean legs eating up the distance between us. My feet are glued to the earth beneath them and it's like going through the storm a second time to have him right in front of me. He hasn't changed a bit in months since I last saw him. If anything, he's even more devastatingly handsome.

Kitted out in a Battleboro Fire and Rescue uniform, he's not only handsome, he's heart-stopping. I'd forgotten how tall he is until he comes to a stop in front of me. Nearly six-two to my five-six, he may as well be a giant. I remember waking up that night after being wrapped up in him and I'd felt so safe and protected. I'd never felt like that before in my life. It's addicting—that feeling of being safe. A girl could learn to get used to having a man make her feel protected. Maybe that's why I'd run.

"Christ, Avery. Is that you? What's wrong? Are you hurt?"

I have to close my eyes hard and pull myself back to the present. "No, it's not me. I'm fine. It's my neighbors. They're trapped inside their house. Can you help?" I want to take the words back as soon as they come out of my mouth, but Mary and Tom need my help. That's all this is. That's all it can be.

"Sure. Lead the way."

I'm hyper aware of him right behind me and my mind is racing the whole walk up to the front door. All I can think is that I need to get away from him as quickly as possible.

"If you'll keep them calm, I'll see if I can get this tree out of their door. Have them stay back just in case."

Nodding, I go to the front window and get as close as I can. "Mary, there's a firefighter here to help. He wants you guys to stay away from the door while he tries to get the block out of the way. Okay?"

"Okay, Avery. You tell him thank you for us!" Mary shouts and then everything is drowned out by the buzzing of the chainsaw.

I back away a few feet, but still stay in view of the front window in case Mary or Tom need me. Naturally, my eyes are drawn to Walker as he attempts to cut the limb down and I can't seem to look away no matter how much I order myself to. His uniform is covered in a fine layer of dust. They must have been working with chainsaws all morning clearing out paths to houses. If the dark circles under his eyes are any indication, he's been at it a while already.

A dozen questions spring to mind. Namely, what the hell he's doing here of all places and why? Then I wonder how long he plans to stay. If he's going back for another contract, I'd prefer he did it sooner rather than later…before things get even more complicated than they already are.

I worry at a nail, biting it down to the quick, as he cuts another divot into the limb. Sweat beads on his forehead and a dark furrow is already soaked into the material of his uniform T-shirt at his back. My mind instantly goes to the identical one I stole from him that I secreted away in my underwear drawer. I take another step away from him to find a pocket of cool air to breathe, but there's none to be found.

The limb gives way with a furious *crack* and Walker heaves it to the side with a strength that has all the feminine parts of me clench up in appreciation. Yes. I definitely need to make a quick getaway. Clearly the months haven't been enough to dull the effect he has on me. Though I'm not sure a decade would be enough time to accomplish that.

Another few minutes and he has the door all clear. Despite my reservations, I really do care about Mary and Tom, so I follow close behind as he sets the chainsaw aside, then knocks and enters. Their living room is a mess of broken glass and debris that Walker and I carefully pick over to where the elderly couple is hovering in their bedroom. Seeing them, I'm reminded of Grandma Rosie and the baby and know I have to get home soon. Grandma Rosie may have moments of lucidity, but she can't be in care of the baby for long.

"Are you two all right?" Walker asks. "I'm with the fire department. Do you need any medical attention?"

He conducts an interview with both of them as I watch, and I'm struck by his competence and efficiency. I've imagined him as a firefighter plenty of times before, but there's something more vulnerable about this aspect of his job that

I'd never considered. There's a humane kindness in his bandaging of a scrape on Mary's forehead and a respectful concern as he takes Tom's heart rate and blood pressure. The fluttering inside me is located decidedly north this time. My heart can't seem to handle watching him care for these people.

"You'll call our daughter for us?" Mary asks for the second time. "She'll come out to get us when the roads are clear enough."

"Yes, ma'am. And I'll come by in the morning with food and water for you. They're supposed to be delivering some from Red Cross, the food banks. Do you have enough to last until then?"

"We'll be fine. We appreciate all your help," Tom answers.

"Any time. I'll see you in the morning."

"You let me know if you need anything before then," I tell Mary.

"Thank you for coming to check on us," she says. "I don't think we ever would have gotten out of here if it wasn't for you."

"Don't you worry about it. That's what neighbors are for. I better go and check on Grandma Rosie."

"You give that baby of yours some sugar for me," Mary calls after me.

My heart leaps into my throat and I glance at the porch to make sure Walker didn't hear her. Thankfully, he's too busy clearing a path down the walk to the driveway to have paid any mind to us.

"I will," I answer Mary and close the door behind me before she can say anything else too revealing.

Walker is probably in town in between contracts again.

Next season when it's time for him to leave, he'll be gone again and that's probably for the best. Or at least that's what I tell myself.

He's waiting for me at the end of their sidewalk, the chainsaw and his kit of supplies at his feet looking like some sort of badass cross between a doctor and a lumberjack. When I get close enough, I open my mouth to say the words that'll put enough distance between us to keep us both in check, but instead he reaches for me in one smooth movement, then crushes me to his body for a kiss as long and steamy as a Florida afternoon.

CHAPTER 5
WALKER

PAST

When I wake up in the middle of the night, it's to the perfume of her pear-scented shampoo filling my nose. It blots out the usual acrid tang of embers and ash and it's so welcome, I press my nose into her hair and breathe deep. She's like the springtime after years of the worst, coldest kind of winter. A cold so deep it almost burns.

She's wrapped up in a little ball in front of me, her legs tucked up into her chest, her hands folded innocently in front of her face. Somehow, I'd wound up wrapped around her with my thighs pressed close against the backs of hers and my chest framing her back. It's been so long since I've had a woman in bed with me, let alone falling asleep with one. I'd forgotten how comforting it can be to simply hold one with all their softness and curves.

If I weren't such a fucked-up man, I'd put some room between us. Even though she'd come back to my place, she doesn't know me. We've never met before tonight and I don't have any claim to her. But that doesn't have any effect on my lizard brain. All it knows is she's sweet and smells good and feels like heaven in my arms.

Reluctantly, I regain control of myself and start to pull away. A hand on my forearm stops me. "No, don't," comes her sleepy voice. "It's nice."

"You don't mind?" I can't see her face to read her expression, but I don't pull away.

"I hope this doesn't sound as weird as I think it does, but I don't get to do this sort of thing a lot. Like, the affection sort of thing."

"I guess that's a good thing to know."

"Why do you say that?"

"That you won't have some angry boyfriend chasing me down."

She puffs out a little laugh. "No, definitely not. I don't really have time outside of work to find any boyfriends, so you're safe."

I relax back into her, tightening my hold around her waist and pressing more closely against her slender body. "I'm the same way. I work a lot, and I'm gone too much for any real kind of relationship. Gotta admit, though, I do miss this sort of thing."

"That's surprising. I would have thought you'd have dozens of women falling at your feet. The whole sexy hero thing you've got going on must be pretty irresistible to them."

With a snort, I say, "Sure, until they realize I'm gone for weeks at a time and can be called away at any second. When I am home, I'm asleep or training. Women don't normally want to stick around when you don't."

There's a moment of silence and then, "I'm sorry. That must be lonely."

I lift a shoulder, then remember we're in the dark. "It can be sometimes, but you stay busy enough to forget. What about you? What keeps you busy outside of work?"

"My grandma. She has Alzheimer's. She has a nurse during the day while I'm at work, but I take care of her pretty much the rest of the time."

"What about your parents? Siblings? They don't help out?"

"My parents passed away when I was younger. They didn't have any other children. My Grandma Rosie and Grandpa Jim raised me. Before he died, I promised him I'd take care of her. It's the least I could do. They were wonderful grandparents to me."

"Your grandma is lucky to have you. I've worked with patients as a paramedic who have Alzheimer's. It's not an easy job."

"It's worth it," Avery says. "I couldn't let her be taken care of by strangers, all confused without anything familiar around. She's lived in the same place pretty much her whole life."

"What would you do if you didn't have to take care of her?"

"I'm not sure. I've never really thought about it. Grandpa Jim got sick right after I graduated. If I had to pick something, maybe teaching? I really like kids."

I smile in the darkness. "Yeah? I could see that. You certainly had more patience last night than I would have."

"You should come on Friday night all you can eat crab legs. It's a madhouse."

"I'll keep that in mind."

"What about you? Have you always wanted to be a firefighter?"

My answer sticks in my throat. Clearing it, I say, "Pretty much. My brother was killed in a fire when I was ten. I guess I've been trying to save him ever since."

"Oh my God, Walker. I'm so sorry."

"It's been a long time."

"Still. I know how it feels. It doesn't ever really go away."

"No, I guess it doesn't."

She turns then, fitting her head underneath my chin. Her free arm goes around my waist and I freeze for a second, unsure. Then, I realize she's giving me a hug and I relax, accepting her feminine strength. I nuzzle my nose back into her hair and let the scent of her shampoo comfort me as much as her arms around me.

I'm not sure who reaches for who first, or maybe we do it at the same time. But somehow our lips find each other in the dark and tangle. There's desperation there, on both our parts. A need to fill a mutual void. A craving for similarities. To know we're not alone with our struggles. She tastes like the vanilla from the coffee, almost too sweet to handle, but I can't stop going back for more. Her groan fills me up and all I want is to hear her do it again and again.

If we only have tonight, then I hope tonight lasts forever.

Avery sheds her clothes as fast as a fox and then makes quick work of mine, too. "Is this okay?" she asks when she reaches for my sweatpants and I choke out a hoarse, "Yes," in response.

I wish there were light so I could get a better look at her. I wish there were more time so I could sample and savor every inch of her. But I'm driven by a desperation to be inside her that's so acute, all I can do is jerk her against my chest and lift one leg over my hip. She reaches between us and positions me, then takes me inside in one smooth motion. Her gasp of pleasure fills the darkness around us as I drive into her obliterating heat.

This isn't how I'd planned for tonight to go. If I was lucky enough to get her into bed, I planned to make it last, make her come at least twice before we got down to business, but I'll be lucky if I don't go off embarrassingly early at this point.

I try to slow down, try to reach between us to get my hands on her so I don't completely ruin this before we've even started, but she pushes my hands away.

"No, don't. You feel so good."

"Baby, if I don't help you out, this is going to be over before it starts."

She writhes against me and her hands dig into my shoulders. "I don't need any help. You're doing just fine."

At that, I give up trying to rein in any sort of control. My fingers bite into her hips and we come together like crashes of thunder in the middle of a storm. Wild and beautiful and unpredictable. She presses close to me like she's trying to climb into my skin. I twist us both so she's on her back. Her arms come around my shoulders, not letting me put any distance between us.

And that's what does it for me, what sends me over the edge. I don't know much about her, but in this moment all I know is she needs me. I couldn't hold back even if I tried. She gasps at the sound of my release and I feel her clench around me a second later, like the physical act of bringing me to the brink is what she needed to get off. If I could come a second time, knowing that would have done it.

We're quiet as our heartbeats slow and our breathing goes

back to normal. I don't want to get up, break the connection, but the orgasm has rendered me exhausted for the second time. She breathes deeply beneath me and I know she's close to falling asleep again, too.

While I'm still conscious, I get up to clean us both up. She murmurs as I wipe away the remnants between her legs and get back into bed. As though we've been doing it for years, she settles back with her ass against my hips and once again the scent of her shampoo lulls me back to a dreamless sleep.

In the morning, I reach for her, but she's gone.

CHAPTER 6
AVERY

My hands go to his biceps to hold on the moment his lips touch mine. The world spins away. I forgot what it's like to feel wanted by him. So many things happened in the months since I've seen him it's easy to push away the memories. The only thing I haven't been able to push away is when he stars in my dreams at night.

Now there's no forgetting the pressure of his lips. There's no washing away his addictive taste. His kiss burns away all my good reason and common sense. If I wasn't hyper aware of every way he invades my senses, I would have said his kiss is another fevered dream.

When his tongue brushes mine it's like I've been stung all over. Nerves that had gone dormant buzz to life like the yellow jackets swarming around us. I make a needy noise in the back of my throat and it's that sound that brings me crashing back to rationality.

My hands are twin vices on his biceps, and I force myself to relax my grip, although very reluctantly. The heat we're generating between us rivals that of the steamy afternoon air. It's a good thing I won't have any hot water when we get home because a cold shower is exactly what I'll need.

"I've been thinking about doing that since the morning I woke up and you weren't there." His rough voice is like honey in my ears.

Hot guilt washes over me. "I'm sorry about that. My grandma was having a moment and I had to leave in a hurry. Besides, I thought it would be easier without the awkward goodbyes."

I make a move to put some space between us, but his hands on my waist tighten, keeping me close. "Would it be creepy of me to say I've thought about you probably more than is healthy while I was gone?"

It's not creepy, but it does hit me right in the heart. I clear my throat. "It's not creepy," I manage to say. In fact, no one has ever said anything of the kind to me before and if I weren't so panicked to have him here in the flesh after all this time, I'd think it was kind of sweet. In the past, what few short-lived relationships I'd cultivated had crashed and burned when they realized how much time I had to devote to Grandma Rosie.

"Why don't we—"

In the distance I hear the squeal of a protesting screen door, cutting off my focus from what Walker's saying. Then the sound of Grandma Rosie's frail voice penetrates my thoughts. "Avery, is that you?"

Before I can say anything, Walker turns and spots Grandma Rosie on the front porch.

He twists back to me for a moment. "Is that your grandma? The one with Alzheimer's?"

My hands grow clammy and I wipe them on my thighs.

"What—what? Oh, um, yes. Grandma Rosie. But she's okay. We didn't have any significant damage and I stocked up before." I'm rambling. I don't know if he can hear the straight panic in my voice, but it sounds brittle and desperate to my ears.

"I should give your place a look before I get back to the guys. It's the least I can do." He gives me one last kiss on the lips and even though it's only the barest touch I feel it down to my bones.

"No!" I nearly shout, but he's already stalking across the street to my house. His long legs make easy work of the distance and I'm simply no match. He's at the fence before I get halfway. The air simply evaporates from my lungs as he eats up the space between the gate and the front door where Grandma Rosie is waiting patiently, innocently. I don't know where the baby is, probably still asleep in the bassinet, but she isn't holding her. With my heart in my throat, I follow behind as quickly as possible.

"Good morning, ma'am, I'm Walker Bryant with the fire department. How are you doing?"

"Has there been a fire?" I hear Grandma Rosie ask.

"No, ma'am. I'm helping with the cleanup after the storm. You remember the storm from last night?"

"Storm?" Grandma Rosie's expression is guileless.

"Yes, ma'am, there was a bad hurricane last night. How are you feeling?"

"Oh, I'm all right. My granddaughter Avery takes good care of me."

Walker glances back over his shoulder at me as I climb the steps to the porch, out of breath. Both from the kiss and the short sprint across the street.

"I bet she does."

"Do you want some sweet tea?" I wince at Grandma Rosie's ingrained hospitality. The last thing I want is for Walker to go inside.

"No, Grandma, I'm sure he's—"

But Walker acts like he doesn't hear me. "That would be great, ma'am, thank you."

I nearly wince. "Are you sure you aren't busy? Don't you have a ton of people to check on or something?"

Walker merely grins over his shoulder as Grandma Rosie leads him inside the house. "I always have time for the company of beautiful women."

My heart is at my feet as we move inside. Rosie busies herself making us all glasses of sweet tea. I already know I won't be able to drink any around the knot in my throat. All I can see are the baby things everywhere. A man like Walker must notice everything, so they can't go outside his observation. Once she gives him the glass of tea, Grandma Rosie smiles and goes back to watching her shows on her tablet in the recliner.

His throat works as he drinks deeply. Despite my panic, my eyes are glued to him. "Have you been working all night?" I figure distracting him will be the next best thing. Maybe if I do, he won't notice the bottles on the counter or the breast pump on the kitchen table. My cheeks burn with embarrassment and I hope he thinks it's because of the heat. I don't know if it's my nerves or the lack of air conditioning, but it feels about 100 degrees inside now.

Walker finishes the glass and sets it inside the sink next to a bottle he doesn't seem to pay any mind to. "Well, I'm between contracts again and I came back to visit. When I heard about the storm, I volunteered with the fire department for their emergency response. When they saw how bad it could be, they knew they needed all the help they could get. It's a mess out there."

"If it's anything like around here, you'll have your work cut out for you." I hope that didn't sound as inhospitable as it does inside my head.

"You're not wrong." With a quick glance at Grandma Rosie, he says, "So would it be okay if I came back the next time I'm free? I'm not sure when that'll be, but I want to see you again. I wanted to see you again after you left, but I didn't have any way to contact you. I never did get your number."

This is either my dreams come true, or my worst nightmare. I'm not certain which.

"Um, I'm not sure—"

Once again, I'm interrupted.

This time, by the thin, high-pitched wail of a hungry baby girl.

CHAPTER 7
WALKER

The first thing that comes to mind is there's a baby at a neighbor's. With most of the electricity out, it's easier to hear ambient noises around even with all of the chainsaws buzzing around. Then I see Avery's pained ghost-white expression. My brows furrow, because the dots don't connect.

She'd never mentioned a kid before and I would have noticed if she had. Without a word, Avery turns and disappears into a bedroom and I'm left in a pile of confusion until she returns with a swaddled, squirming bundle in her hands. Throughout the paramedic arm of my training, I've been around enough babies to know a newborn or thereabouts when I see one and that baby isn't more than a month or two old.

Avery doesn't meet my eyes as she retrieves a container of milk from a cooler. She prepares the bottle in the absolute quiet save for the fussing sounds from the infant. The baby quiets as she teases its mouth with the bottle and begins to eat.

I don't know what to think at first. My mind goes incredibly blank. After some quick mental calculations, I realize either she was pregnant when we were together or…

No.

There's no way.

She would have found a way to tell me.

I couldn't have spent nearly an entire year as a—I nearly choke on my own spit at the thought that follows—father and not known it.

"Is that a baby?" I ask when I can finally get my voice to work again.

Avery's eyes are still on the gurgling infant and she nods silently.

"Look at me," I demand, my heartbeat throbbing throughout my entire body. I swear I can almost hear it pounding in my head and ears. When she doesn't, I say, "Avery."

Her wide eyes meet mine reluctantly and there's fear and defiance there in equal measure. "This is Rosalynn Grace," she says. "My daughter. Gracie."

"When was she born?" My words come out as harsh and choppy as the ocean in the middle of a winter storm.

"A few months ago." Her words are so faint I damn near have to read her lips to know what she's saying.

It doesn't take a genius to realize a few months plus nine months gestation means the baby was conceived roughly the same time we were together. The sweet tea turns sour in my stomach and the sugar now seems like a terrible idea. I want to sit down, but I'm afraid if I try to move, my locked knees will give out from underneath me, completely betraying the level of shock I'm experiencing.

"Is she mine?" I ask, the words coming out harsh and

cold unintentionally. Or maybe the tone is intentional. How could she have kept a secret like this from me for so long? What if something had happened to me and I didn't make it out of a fire alive and died not knowing I had a child out there in the world.

At my question, Avery's eyes go back to the now sleeping baby's face. Mine follow despite how much I try to keep from looking at them, feeling anything for them. The baby must sense some of the unease in the room, because she shifts restlessly, her sleepy eyes cracking open just long enough for me to see how identical they are to my own.

"Yes," is all Avery says.

At her answer, I collapse into the chair at the table next to her, my thoughts racing. I have a daughter. The words repeat over and over until they have no real meaning. *I have a daughter.*

I'd never given much thought to children. I never had much time. If I wasn't training or fighting fires, I was traveling back and forth to Battleboro to make sure what was left of my family didn't splinter off and fall to ruin. There was never any room for starting a family.

"Why didn't you tell me?" I demand.

Her hand fiddles with the baby's blanket and a little chubby arm breaks free of its restraints and a pudgy hand finds her fingers and holds on tight. I can't say why the image makes my chest tighten, but it does.

"You were already gone. I tried to find you, but I barely knew you. I only found out your last name today because you told Mary and Tom."

"You knew I was from Battleboro. It's not a small town, but you could have asked around if you wanted to and someone would have pointed you in the right direction."

She bites her lip and I notice how red it is, nearly raw to the touch, from her constant gnawing. "I could have tried harder," she admits, faltering. "I take full blame for that. I was scared."

It's her breathless vulnerability that stops me from berating her further. Striving for calm, I say, "I've had a daughter for damn near a year and you couldn't tell me because you were scared? Do I seem like that much of a jerk to you?"

Her eyes widen. "No!" Her raised voice jolts a cry out of the baby. As Avery tries to soothe her, she says, "No, of course not. I just—I could hear how much you loved what you do. I could never take that from you. I knew you'd be back eventually and each day I didn't tell you I rationalized that maybe it was better this way if you didn't know."

"That wasn't your decision to make. I had a right to know."

Who knows what the hell I would have done with the knowledge, but now I'll never get the chance to find out.

"You did. I know you did. It was wrong of me and I'm sorry. I was scared."

"Of what? Of me?"

"No, of course not. Of a lot of things. She means everything to me. I thought I was doing what was best for her." The words sound torn from her very soul and I have to fight not to reach for her, bite back the words of consolation.

My first instinct is to soothe, but anger overrides it. "Do you have a police scanner?"

She glances up, confusion written on her face. "A— what?"

"A police scanner. Do you have one?"

"Um, I think so. My grandpa used to volunteer at the fire

department. He liked to listen to it sometimes and I kept it around because listening to it reminds me of him." Her expression turns wary. "Why do you ask?"

I get to my feet, suddenly needing some space. "Because that's how we're communicating. You can listen to them for the most up to date information and to find out when they're organizing distribution of resources or whatever. Where's your phone?"

She blows out a breath, her brows still knitted with confusion. Pulling the phone out of her pocket, she says, "It doesn't really work."

I program my number into hers, then send myself a text from her phone so I have it stored in mine. "Texts do, but they take a little longer. If you three run into an emergency, you can shoot me a text and I'll be here as soon as I can. Do you have access to a generator? It's gonna get hot soon and that baby and your grandma will need cool air."

"No, not yet, but I—"

"If you don't have one by tomorrow, I'll have one delivered here. Is there anything else you need?"

"No, I think we're okay. But you don't have to go to the trouble. I planned to get one as soon as I could."

"I'll take care of it. Keep your phone and the police scanner nearby. I put in the numbers for the station if you need to get ahold of me and can't get to me with my cell."

"You don't have to go to all this trouble."

I shoulder my kit and head back through the house without answering. I'm not sure I can without spewing a ton of nasty thoughts and I'm not the sort to pop off without considering my words. Her footsteps follow close behind and I can feel the anxious waves of energy emanating off of her at my back.

"I'm sorry," she says when I reach the door.

I jerk my head in answer. I have nothing else left in me to say. Nothing nice anyway.

CHAPTER 8
AVERY

True to his word, a generator magically appears on my porch the following day. The only note with it are instructions on how to set it up safely. Apparently several people have already been killed by having the exhaust blow into their homes and causing them to slowly asphyxiate. The generator also runs on gas so there were an additional five cans of gas lined up like neat little soldiers.

I didn't plan to run the generator constantly, mostly through the hottest part of the afternoon because there was no telling how long the electricity would be down. From what reports I'd heard over the police scanner and the spotty connections I'd made on my phone I'd gleaned power lines were down from Mexico Beach to Tallahassee. It would take months of repairs and thousands of linemen from all over the country to repair the catastrophic damage.

You know your shit has gone sideways when the aftermath of a hurricane is easier to deal with than the wreck of your personal life.

In the long days that follow, I spend most of my time

trying to get the front yard in some semblance of order. I learn through the patchwork communication grapevine that there will be debris pickups on certain days of the week if the community puts the debris on the side of the road. When I'm not taking care of Grandma Rosie or tending to the baby, I'm hauling limbs and logs to the ever-growing pile by the road. I borrow a spare chainsaw from Tom and after a quick lesson, get to work cutting down some of the more manageable felled limbs. There are a few monsters I don't know what I'll do with, probably pay someone to remove at some point, but that'll have to be put off until later.

It's a lot of work, but it keeps my mind off of Walker and gives me something to do since most roads are still closed unless you're getting food from the various distribution locations or getting gas for your generator. There's even a curfew for our town to discourage looters. Someone had tried to open our front door a few days after the storm, but our automatic porch flood lights scared them away. It's the only time I've ever wished I had a gun in the house, but thankfully I haven't had to resort to that.

All in all, it could be so much worse. The only tree that fell on the house was an immature magnolia and it didn't cause any structural damage. I was able to get it cut down for the most part. There's still the base of it sticking out at an angle across the yard, but at least it's not on the roof. The others that were blown down were in the back yard and out of the way. Most of the damage to the house was the window that was broken and some of the tin that was pulled up by the wind. Truthfully, we got lucky.

So, so lucky.

I've seen pictures of homes in our area that were completely wiped away. Roofs ripped completely off. Trees spearing through living rooms, through cars. That's not to mention the homes on the coast where the hurricane made landfall. The whole community of Mexico Beach…there aren't words to describe the devastation. My family and I have spent many summers swimming at Mexico and Panama City Beach. To many Floridians in the Panhandle, they're as ingrained in your blood as choosing a side in the Florida / Florida State rivalry. Seeing the pictures of entire tracts of homes simply wiped away…there's no way to explain the hole it leaves. I can't imagine how that would feel to the people who live there. Lived there.

It's hard enough seeing images from my own town. Entire forests wiped out. Whole landscapes marred for the foreseeable future. The world I grew up in has forever been changed. My daughter will never know the Florida I grew up in and there's a bracing somberness to accepting that.

About two weeks after the storm, when I'm certain Walker has completely written me off, I wake up to the sound of a chainsaw close by. It's not an uncommon occurrence at this point—the chorus of chainsaws is almost comforting now—but this one sounds like it's right outside my door. It wakes the baby, too, so I nurse her back to a contented state and entertain her with a few toys clipped to a bouncer. She's more awake these days, so I try to tire her out a bit before I put her back to sleep.

While she's distracted, I take care of Grandma Rosie, getting her fed and making sure she takes all of her medication. Once that's done, I can finally investigate the source of the sound, which has now moved to the backyard. Hesitantly, I open the door and find a shirtless, sweaty Walker cutting down the fallen trees crisscrossing the property.

Stunned, a little confused, and a whole lot turned on, all

I can do is watch as he works. The strong patchwork of muscles covering his back flex and contract with every movement. The sheen of sweat emphasizes each curve and bulge. He pauses to drink from a water bottle and uses the remnants to spray over his body, making him look like a real-life Chippendale's commercial. The sight of the water makes me realize my throat has gone dry and if it weren't for that, I'd be drooling.

Turning, he spots me standing on the back porch ogling him. The chainsaw cuts off, leaving a deafening silence in its wake. I swallow back my apprehension and put a damper on the raging hormones that had roared to life the moment they saw him.

"What are you doing?" I ask in a neutral tone, my voice raised to cover the distance.

He lifts the chainsaw in a gesture toward the tree. "Cutting down this tree for you."

I lift a brow. "I can see that. I guess the more appropriate question would be *why* are you cutting it down?"

"Because I had the time and the ability. Are you complaining about it?" There's a hard twist to his mouth I haven't seen before. So he hasn't forgiven me yet, not that I thought he would. He has a right to be bitter, mad, disappointed or maybe all of the above.

"No, I'm just wondering why. You don't have to do these things for us."

"What things?"

I wave a hand to our surroundings. "You don't have to get us a generator and gas or clear out my backyard. Those things aren't your responsibility."

"Like you didn't think a baby was my responsibility."

"That's not fair."

"I think in this circumstance, I'll get to decide what's fair." He props the chainsaw on the tree stump and moves closer to me. "I've had a lot of time to think over the past few weeks and I think what pisses me off the most is that you made the decision for me about one of the most important things that can happen in a man's life. That wasn't fair. You don't get to make that choice for someone else."

I don't know if it's the hormones, the heat, or the sting of righteous condemnation in his eyes, but I find my own temper rising. "That's what being a parent is all about. You think I didn't agonize about not trying harder to find you and let you know? It's all I thought about since I found out I was pregnant. But it wasn't about me and it wasn't about you. I had to do what I thought was best for my daughter. I've been through the loss of a parent. I didn't want to do that to her."

His eyes flash. "And what makes you think she'd have to lose me?"

"Look at your job! You jump into fires for a living, Walker. You're gone most of the time and there could be a day when you don't come back. What kind of life is that for a child? Would you want that for her?" When he doesn't answer, I push on. "It was that indecision that kept me from trying harder. That and we didn't know each other! We only spent one night together. How was I supposed to know the right thing to do? I made a mistake. I'm human. I promise I'm going to make more of them. Becoming a parent will surely teach you that." Striving for calm, I continue, "But I want to make things right. I want you to meet her. To figure out what you want your place in her life to be. Whatever that is, we'll deal with it and I promise as long as you're in our lives, I won't ever keep anything from you again."

When he says, "Are you done?" I nearly impale him with the chainsaw.

Instead, I gesture for him to speak before I commit a felony.

"I don't know where you and I go from here." I can't hide my wince at that, but it's what I was expecting. "But I do know I want the chance to figure this out. I never planned on having a family, for the reasons you listed and more, but she's here and she's mine. I owe it to her and to me to see exactly what that means."

I know if I don't say the words then I never will, so I blurt, "And us?"

His gaze meets mine. The spark I felt when we first met blazes to life between us. Sensing it, he takes a step back and I can't deny that hurts. "I don't know about us. I think we should take this slow and focus on one thing at a time. The baby—what did you say her name was?"

"Rosalynn, for my grandma. Rosalynn Grace. I mostly call her Gracie, though."

"Gracie," he murmurs, his eyes a little misty. "Well, Gracie deserves our attention now."

I know this is progress, I know I should be happy, but I can't help but feel like I've lost something that could have been amazing.

CHAPTER 9
WALKER

"I'm not sure if I ever really thanked you for the generator. It was really a lifesaver. I think Grandma Rosie would have melted without it." Her shy little smile throws me back to the night we met. How I thought I'd do anything just to see her aim that smile in my direction. "So thank you, really. I appreciate it more than you know."

"You're welcome, but I bet you're happy to have electricity back on." I pass Gracie from one arm to another. For a baby, she certainly has some chunk on her. She grins toothlessly at me and I find myself smiling back down at her. My family and I aren't close anymore. I come back to Battleboro to check on them because I imagine it's what my brother would want me to do so the feelings of love and connection I feel so quickly for this little girl simply astound me. "Aren't you Gracie-girl?"

"More than you know. Do they have power restored where you're at?" Avery asks.

"Last week. I have to tell you, it was nice taking a hot shower again." I don't say that I'm almost sad about it.

Restoring utilities, getting most of the roads cleared for the most part, it means I won't be as needed here. The fire department is already scaling back hours for the volunteers. I never thought I'd say it, but I almost like the small crew of down-to-earth guys there. A far cry from the egos I'm used to.

"Agreed. Cold ones are fun when it's ninety degrees outside, but I missed bubble baths. Now if only we could get internet back up and running."

I try not to think about Avery naked and covered in bubbles. I try and fail. "They still haven't gotten yours fixed?"

Avery smiles sadly. "No, and they said it could be months, but I guess that's to be expected. Data is working faster on our phones and tablets, but they throttle it in the evenings, so everything runs as slow as a turtle."

"You know you can always come to my place. Mine is back up." And maybe I like the thought of her, the baby and even Grandma Rosie with me doing things like the dishes and watching her grandma's trash T.V.

At this, she pauses gathering the dishes from lunch. "Thank you. That's nice of you to offer."

"It's no problem. I'm hardly ever there anyway."

"Is the fire department still going door to door?"

That's not the reason I'm never there. It's because I can't stand the quiet. It's why I'm always here when I'm not working or training. "Not so much anymore." Gracie coos and gnaws on a teether in my lap. Avery says I'm crazy, but I'm almost positive she's going to be popping out some teeth soon. "We're mostly working on a volunteer basis to get more roads cleared out. When do you go back to work?"

"Monday, unfortunately. I've been enjoying the time off to spend with Gracie and Grandma Rosie, but with the restaurant opening back up—finally—I can't put it off anymore. They won't hold off on demanding payment on bills forever. I just hate that I have to send Gracie girl back to daycare."

Studying the baby in my arms, I find myself saying, "Why don't you let me watch her?"

Avery pauses in drying a plate. "Really? You want to do that?"

"If you don't mind. I think it'd probably be a good idea for us to spend some more time together. You work the evenings, right?" At her nod, I say, "That's perfect. I can switch around for the day shift and watch Gracie at night when you work."

At her look, I say, "What?"

"Are you sure? I can't imagine you dealing with diapers and bottles all day."

"And you know me so well," I say and she pauses for a minute before realizing I'm teasing.

"Ha, ha, very funny," she says and flings a handful of soap bubbles at me. "I mean you do know infant CPR, so that's a plus."

"Then what is it?" I ask.

"I guess I'm realizing that you were serious when you said you wanted to make this work. I figured you'd get bored after a while and need some action." At my lifted brow, she says, "Not that kind of action. I mean like a burning building or a pileup or something."

"You make me out to be more of a daredevil than I am."

"Right so jumping out of planes isn't because you like the adrenaline. Then why do you do it?"

I lift a shoulder. "Why do people do anything? I guess it started with a morbid fascination after my brother was killed in a fire and grew from there. Fighting fires is something I can control, believe it or not. It's the rest of the world that goes a little mad sometimes."

"You don't miss it?"

"You mean to imply that a category five hurricane isn't enough action for me?"

She leans against the counter, all hips and dark hair that tumbles down her shoulders. "Touché I guess. What time works for you?"

Babies aren't as easy as they look. Sure, they sleep most of the time, but they spend a good portion of the rest of it crying. Give me a fire any day and I can take charge and get it put out, but a crying baby? May as well be the world's most complicated Sudoku.

"C'mon, girl. What's wrong?" I check her diaper. Still clean and dry. She just had a bottle not five minutes ago and I've bounced and rocked her so much my arms ache—and I'm used to carrying rucksacks that weigh upward of fifty pounds on a light day. "You can't be hungry. You aren't sick, are you?"

That would go over well with Avery, I'm sure. The first day back at work and I tap out because the baby has a cold. I press my hand against Gracie's forehead. She's warm, but not hot. She drools on my hand and I wipe it away.

"Don't worry, girl. I won't take offense."

Her gummy smile reminds me of my thought about her teething. I grab a piece of ice and put it in a clean rag for her to suck on. It's like magic. In an instant, she stops crying and goes to town gnawing on the cold rag. Avery is going to flip her shit. *Babies aren't supposed to get teeth this early* my ass.

"See there? We can do this. It'll just take some learning for the both of us. What do you think, Gracie-girl? You think you'd like to have me as a dad?"

At my question, she looks up from her chewing to smile at me again. I'm filled with twin shards of delight and guilt. Her smile is a carbon copy of Avery's, but her eyes? They're all mine. I don't need the DNA test we'd taken to confirm paternity to know she's mine. I knew the moment I saw her. To have her smiling at me? It's the world's best Christmas present and winning the lottery all in one.

But there's guilt there, too. Guilt because a part of me knows Avery wasn't far off the mark when she said I needed the thrill, that my job is dangerous. I won't deny both of those reasons are why I love being a Wildland Firefighter so much. If I do decide to stick around, could I give those things up? Much as I want to think I'd be the selfless parent that Avery is, I'm not sure I could.

CHAPTER 10
AVERY

I'll be the first to admit, I had my doubts about Walker. Clearly.

But when the first night of babysitting—or rather I should say parenting—didn't end in absolute disaster, I have to admit, I was wrong. Gracie was happy and healthy when I went to pick her up after my shift and Walker didn't even seem frazzled. I guess when you compare it to a wildfire, watching after one baby can't really be that intimidating.

We continue with this routine for the next couple of weeks. He spends more and more of his free time cleaning up the rest of the larger debris in my yard. In no time he has the large fallen trees hacked to pieces and burned. He even climbs up on top of my roof and replaces the tin that had gotten torn up when I told him it was leaking inside the house during the next rainstorm.

The be-all and end-all, though, is when he's with Gracie. If I had no feelings for him after our night together, seeing him with our daughter would have done it for me. He was awkward at first, a little unsure, but the two of them have a rapport I don't think I'll ever be able to attain. He's light-hearted and daring, letting her grab onto his fingers to practice her wobbly legs and cheering her on while I bite my nails off. He lights up when he sees her and the more time I spend with him, the harder it is for me to remember why I shouldn't want anything more than a father for my daughter.

Before we can blink, it's nearly Christmas time. I insisted he spend the night so he could be there for Gracie's first Christmas morning. How could I not? Seeing him watching her would be the best Christmas gift I've ever received.

If I thought he was good-looking in a pair of cut-offs and a T-shirt, it was only because I hadn't seen him in a flannel and jeans. Or even worse, a Christmas onesie that matches the drooling giggling baby girl in his arms. "You're sure you don't mind?"

I give myself a mental shake. Must stop picturing him stripping for me. That's not exactly the platonic coparenting relationship we agreed on. "I'm sure."

"I can just drive over in the morning."

He has Gracie in his lap. He's staring down at her as she coos and waves her arms. The look on his face is indescribable as he babbles at her like they're having a full-blown conversation. It's like I don't even exist. I've never been so happy to be ignored in my life. I can't believe I thought it would hurt her to have him in her life. If anyone knows what it's like to be without a parent, it's me.

After clearing my throat, I say, "I said I was sure. Geez, Walker, are you going deaf already? You can borrow some of Grandma Rosie's hearing aids."

"Fine," he replies with an exaggerated expression which

causes Gracie to giggle up at him. Be still my heart. He places her in her bouncer to kick and play with the toys hanging over her. "I'll stay, but I'm sleeping on the couch."

I nearly roll my eyes. "Really, like we haven't shared a bed before."

At this, his gaze turns molten and the air between us heats like we're creating our own personal wildfire. "Right. And remember what happened the last time?"

My cheeks burn. We'd been dancing around each other for weeks. The sexual tension hadn't gone away because we'd decided to be mommy and daddy. It had only gotten worse, at least for me, because I knew making a move would be a huge mistake. "Fine. Stay on the couch."

But my words come out way more breathless than I'd like. Instead of joking back with me, Walker says nothing. His eyes drop to my lips and I can feel his gaze like he's kissing me again—something he hadn't done since the first day. Something I'd been thinking about damn near every second since.

Grandma Rosie is napping and Gracie is happily kicking away in her bouncer, but it feels like Walker and I are the only two people in the world. It's the same way he'd made me feel the first night I met him at the restaurant. It had been crowded then with the dinner rush, but the second we locked eyes, everything else faded away. I used to make fun of women who talked about love at first sight. Okay, maybe it was lust at first sight and love the moment I saw Gracie smiling up at him.

I'd been hit on at work before, but it didn't feel that way with Walker. He hadn't hit on me, not really. At the end of my shift, he'd asked me to a nearby bar, no pretense, no phony coaxing, and I'd said yes without hesitation. I've asked myself a thousand times why? What made him feel so safe?

Now I know.

It had been his eyes. They'd been so achingly sad and lonely. Not in a pitiful, I'll be your female knight-in-shining-armor kind of way. More in an I've found my likeness in another sort of way. In his eyes, I saw my own loneliness reflected and for a moment, maybe I thought…it's silly now, but maybe I thought he'd understand how that felt.

I wonder if he can read how much I want him in my eyes just as easily. The air between us seems to crackle with potential. Potential for heat. For more. Potential for heartbreak. The tension sizzles along my skin, taking with it what little self-control I'd cultivated.

Giving in, I lift my hand to his chest and nearly shiver at the mere feeling of his warmth underneath my palm. I've spent so many nights since he kissed me after the storm reliving the moment and wishing I'd let myself enjoy it more that my knees nearly buckle at the contact. Underneath my palm, his heart beats in an unsteady gallop and I wonder if he's thought about touching me as much as I have him.

I look up and his blue-gray eyes have gone stormy dark. His lips are slightly parted and his chest lifts rapidly with each inhalation. My stomach clenches with the knowledge that I'm not the only one who has been tortured by the distance. I'm not the only one who has been suffering with needs long repressed.

"We should put the baby down for bed," he says in a rough voice. "So she gets enough sleep for tomorrow."

"She's fine," I say with a shake of my head.

"Avery," he warns.

But for the first time in my life, I don't heed the warnings. Don't follow the rules. I lift up to the tips of my toes to reach his lips and kiss him like I've been wanting to kiss him since I first saw him. His hands come to my hips, but they don't push me away. Instead, they grip and hold as though he's afraid to let me go, too.

A bud of hope takes place in my chest as his lips part for me and his tongue flits out to caress my own. The hands at my hips tighten almost to the point of pain, but I don't care. All I want is to drown in him for a little while longer. He retreats, but only to rub his lips over mine, to tease and tempt. I push myself up higher, riddled with need, which makes him laugh.

"Don't laugh," I say indignantly. "Just kiss me."

"So impatient," he teases and pleases us both by bringing his mouth back to mine.

This kiss is deeper and longer. It brings to mind tangled sheets and slick skin. If kissing him was a mistake, it's one I want to make over and over and over again.

I don't know who made the first move, but the next thing I know I'm beneath him on the threadbare couch. He feels so good on top of me it almost makes me want to climb out of my own skin because the wanting him is so intense. His hands are all over me, restless with his own urgency. My thighs part to bring him closer and I hiss my pleasure at the contact. All I can think about is that I want more.

The baby chooses that moment to start crying.

Walker freezes above me, his head popping up in disbelief. My body goes limp with frustration and I press my hands to my face to fight for some semblance of self-control. With careful movements, he gets to his feet.

"I'll get her," he says.

I'm grateful for the moment to myself to put the needy parts of me back together again. I'd been close, so close, to the edge and he'd barely even touched me. If I thought it would be easy to do this co-parenting thing without making it complicated, I knew now I was dead wrong.

CHAPTER 11
WALKER

"We need to talk."

No one likes to hear those words, but I'd been expecting them ever since we kissed the night before Christmas. We'd been able to toe around the tension between us while we focused on Gracie, but her kissing me changed everything. "I know. Did Gracie go down?" I ask.

"For the count." Avery settles on the couch next to me. It's two days past Christmas, but I couldn't seem to make myself leave. Opening presents with Gracie, Rosie, and Avery had been the kind of holidays I'd never gotten as a child after my brother died. Maybe I wanted to soak up as much of it as possible, not that Avery seemed to mind.

Until now.

She didn't object when I suggested I stay the night—on the couch—to help with Grandma Rosie once she caught a nasty cold after the holiday. In fact, part of her seemed relieved. Maybe she thought I'd run at the first opportunity. Maybe she wanted me to stick around. At this point, I didn't know which option I preferred. Both equally scare the shit out of me.

"What did you need to talk about?"

"You've been avoiding me," Avery says directly.

I've learned since I've been around her that keeping things to herself is an aberration. She must have been truly scared to withhold the truth about Gracie for so long—not that that's an excuse. In her day-to-day life Avery tackles her responsibilities head on which includes any confrontations. I won't ever forget that she lied by omission, but I can understand her reasoning more. Or at least her state of mind when she did what she did.

"I've been less than twenty feet away from you for nearly a week."

Avery rolls her eyes. "Don't play dumb. It was the kiss, wasn't it? Did it make it too weird? Look, I'm sorry for coming on to you if that's not what you wanted. The last thing I want to do is to make this harder on anyone. Gracie is the only one who matters here and if you meant it about putting our parenting relationship first, then I'll respect that from this point forward. I know you may not have forgiven me for what I did, I mean I understand—"

I press my fingers over her lips and bite back a smile. God, she loves to ramble when she gets all worked up. I didn't know that about her. There are so many things I don't know about her. So many things I wish I could learn about her. "I've forgiven you."

She deflates a little, then says, "You have?"

Nodding, I drop my fingers and say, "I've seen how hard it is for you to work, take care of your grandma and take care of Gracie. You're a good mom, Ave, and I can accept that you were scared of how I'd react. We never really knew each other, and it was a crazy situation to be put in. I can't say how I'd react if something similar happened to me, so I have no right to judge you. I'm not going to lie and say it doesn't hurt having missed everything, but I'm willing to work with you to move forward."

"Wow, that's not what I was expecting you to say," she says with a laugh. "Thank you. I hope you know I mean that. You've done so much for us already and—"

"Stop, you don't have to keep thanking me. I do those things because I want to."

She gestures over her lips with a zipping motion.

"There's something I need to talk to you about, too."

I wasn't sure how I was going to bring this up. I'd spent the past few days since I learned about it to decide what I wanted to do, and I figure I'd better get it over with before I lose my nerve.

Her smile falls. "What is it?"

"I got offered a job."

She brightens a little. "At the fire department?"

Well, I had, but I couldn't tell her that. Shaking my head, I say, "No, another contract. This one for nearly double what I usually work and what's basically a promotion. It's something I've been working for my whole life."

"You did? A promotion, wow. You must be really hot stuff, huh?" Her expression is a mixture of surprise, pain, and false happiness.

Somehow, it's worse that she's trying so hard to be happy for me. Indecision chokes my words, but I say, "Yeah, I apply for them every year. The listings normally don't go up for a few months, but I wasn't sure how we, this, everything was going to work out, so when I saw it, I applied as a contingency."

Her smile is kind and understanding, which shouldn't feel like a knife to the heart, but it does. "You don't have to explain yourself. I know I was emotional about your job in the beginning, but I can't be mad at you for doing something you love. I saw you after the storm. I could never be so calm and brave like you were. If this is what you want to do, it would be wrong of me not to support you. You're a great firefighter, Walker. A good person. Gracie will always be proud to call you her dad."

I slump back against the couch. "What made you change your mind?"

"Well, I've seen you with Gracie and I can't deny you're so good with her. Even though you may not be the type of dad who's there every day, you're a man she can be proud to call her father and that matters more than anything to me. I was wrong. I had no right to dictate what your relationship would be. If you want to fight wildfires every year, I'm sure we can figure out a way to make your relationship with Gracie when you're here the best it can be."

"Do you really mean that?" I can't tell from her expression or her voice what she's feeling. No doubt she's drawing from that well of inner strength—or maybe that's my vanity talking. And then I feel like shit. I shouldn't want her to be upset that I'm leaving.

"I wouldn't say it if I didn't."

"What about us?"

At this, she pulls away and I feel the distance settle between us like a rock. "I think you were right. What's most important is that you and Gracie have a positive relationship. I don't ever want to come between you two or you following your dreams."

"What if I said I wanted to make it work? All of it?"

"How would we do that?" she asks.

"Well, we could start by going out on an actual date."

To my relief, she laughs, but her eyes are somber. "If we did that eventually you would feel obligated to stay and you would start to resent me. Or I'd get insecure about you being away so much. I don't want that to sour anything and affect your wanting to be with Gracie."

"Nothing would ever affect my wanting to be with Gracie. I'll admit, at first my instinct was to bolt. I've run from being tied down like this my whole life. My father never got over being married and not chasing his dreams. When we lost my brother, it damn near broke him and I swore I'd never fall into that trap."

"Exactly," Avery says. "I don't want you to try and stay for me. Whatever you do, we'll make sure Gracie gets time with you. When you're off season or on vacation when she's older, she can visit or stay with you when she's in town."

There's a glint in her eye and for the first time I don't think I'm going to be able to convince her otherwise when she has her mind set. "Is this really what you want?"

"I only want you to be happy. If this contract makes you happy, I think you should take it. I won't ever stand in your way of doing what you love, Walker."

The hardest thing I've ever done was walk away from the two of them the next morning knowing I wouldn't be seeing them again for a long, long time.

Then realizing if shit went sideways, it could be the last time I ever saw them.

CHAPTER 12
AVERY

If I had any doubts about how the short time with Walker had affected Gracie, they're extinguished by how cranky she is in the days following his departure. She may only be a baby, but she can certainly tell when her world is not as it should be.

I rock her back and forth, jiggling her in my arms and shh-ing with all my might, but nothing helps. Like me, she'd gotten used to having him around and now she doesn't like it when he's gone. Her face is flushed red and angry tears leak from the corners of her eyes. Nothing has ever made me feel as helpless, not even being in the middle of a hurricane, as not being able to comfort my baby.

Kissing her forehead, I murmur, "I understand, honey-bee, but Daddy had to go fight fires. He'll be back in a few months to see you. He promised."

I'd come to the realization after we kissed that if I truly cared for Walker like I thought I did, then that meant I had to give him the space to come to terms with being a father on his own. I couldn't force a happy relationship with Gracie—

or with me—not after I'd stolen it from him in the first place. I would do my best to facilitate, but it would be up to him.

"It's the right decision," I tell the fussing baby. "You'll understand when you're older. God, what a total mom thing to say."

Eventually, she settles down into a fitful sleep on my chest. I park myself on the couch to give us both some rest before my next shift at work. Gracie will be going back to the evening daycare, which I'm already dreading, but it is what it is. Life goes on. As evidenced by the healing community around me every day, life goes on, but only if you put in the effort.

Gracie fights me at drop-off, and I arrive at the restaurant already ready to go home. I'm not in the mood for the rude, entitled customers or the grabby hands, but I have a baby to raise and Grandma Rosie's night nurse isn't cheap, even after her insurance pays their portion.

Life goes on.

The thought rolls around in my brain over and over.

Life goes on.

Before Walker, I was passing through the days and weeks and years, just trying to keep my head above water. That one night with him had been like a buoy, reminding me I didn't always have to struggle through it alone. Even through the trials of pregnancy and birth, I'd held on to the feeling of having his arms around me, protecting me. Sheltering me. It's the safest I've ever felt.

I shake my head and try to clear it of thoughts of him. My eyes catch on a customer and I nearly do a double take until I realize I'm not seeing things. Either Walker has a twin or he's sitting at the same table he'd been at the night we first met.

Still thinking I'm dreaming, I walk toward him in a daze. "Walker?"

His mouth lifts in a half grin, no doubt at my dumbfounded expression. "You look surprised to see me."

Surprised doesn't cover half of it. I'm still not certain I'm not hallucinating. Gracie has been teething, so sleep has become a thing of the past. Hallucinations wouldn't be outside the realm of possibility. "W-what are you doing here? You're supposed to be halfway to Colorado by now. Is everything okay?"

"Everything's fine." He pulls me down into the chair next to him. Well, I felt his hands on mine. They felt real enough. So he's not a sleep-deprived hallucination, but still, I'm left with more questions than answers.

"Then what are you doing here?" My brain can't quite catch up with reality. Much like the day after the storm when he'd appeared out of nowhere, my thoughts seem to keep misfiring. "Was your flight canceled?"

At this he smiles again, which doesn't help my cognition one bit. "No, it wasn't canceled. I didn't get on it."

"You're not making any sense. Explain it to me in small words because I'm afraid I may be having comprehension issues. I thought it was what you wanted. Why wouldn't you get on the plane? You said yourself you worked for it your whole life. It's everything you ever wanted." I don't know why I'm arguing—having him back is all I've been thinking about since he left. After what I put him through, though, I can't fathom the thought of being the reason he walks away from something he loves so much.

"It's just a job. If it was everything I ever wanted, it wouldn't have felt so wrong taking it. Besides, before I left the fire department here offered me a position. Hell, they're hurting for bodies now they practically begged me to take it."

"I don't understand," I admit with a shake of my head. "Working at a small-town fire department isn't the same as jumping out of planes into wildfires. Would that even make you happy?"

He lifts a hand to cup my nape and warmth spreads all over me. I didn't think I'd ever feel that safe, protective warmth again. When I can meet his eyes again it's through a haze of tears in mine. "It took the time without you to realize I don't want to be anywhere if you and Gracie aren't there."

I can't help the smile that spreads over my lips. Then I frown, demanding through a voice laced think with tears, "Don't play with me unless you mean it."

"I'm not messing with you. I mean it. Following my dreams doesn't mean anything if I do it alone. It's just going through the motions. I'm staying here in Battleboro. I want to be with you and Gracie."

"Wait. Wait. You don't have to do this because you think you have to. I told you I'd make your relationship with Gracie work. You don't have to give up everything for me."

"I'm not giving up anything. Having a life with you and Gracie—that's everything. That means more to me than any job."

"Are you sure?"

He leans forward, kisses my objections away. "I've never been more sure of anything in my life."

Later after the longest shift of my life, Walker pulls me into the house and shuts the front door behind me. Grandma Rosie is long since asleep and Gracie is knocked out after the ride back from daycare, so they aren't disturbed when I giggle as he pushes me against the door and takes my mouth in a hot, sweet kiss.

"This is what I was hoping you'd do the night we met," he says against my lips as fire burns me up from the inside out. "It was killing me not getting to taste you."

His lips travel down my throat, making my reply breathless and desperate. "I wanted to so bad, but I chickened out." His mouth finds mine again and I pant when he breaks free. "What else did you want to do?" I ask, wanting to torture us both a little. It's been a long time…too long, but I want to make it last.

Walker grins wickedly. "Why don't I show you instead?"

My throat goes bone dry. All I can do is nod my assent.

He leads me back to my room on the back side of the house where he patiently, competently strips me of my clothes. Spreading me out before him, he crouches between my legs like a man at a feast. My fingers fist in the comforter as his mouth explores the delicate flesh. My thighs begin to shake at his careful ministrations. When I attempt to vise his head with my legs, his strong fingers clamp down on the trembling muscles and hold me wide for his attention.

"Please," I beg.

But if he hears me, he pays no mind. Clearly he also wants to torture us both a little…or a lot.

I toss and turn as he brings me to the edge and back again several times. It's the most exquisite kind of torture. When I'm coated in a fine sheen of sweat, he finally pulls away to yank off his shirt and tug off his pants. Gloriously naked and hard, he climbs on top of me, fitting between my legs like he was made to be there.

When he slides inside me, it feels like coming home, like I'd been waiting for this moment since the morning when I'd left him asleep in that bed.

His fingers comb through my hair to grip my scalp and he says, "Look at me. I want you to look at me for this." I think he means to look at him when I come, because *God* I'm close, but then he says, "I love you, Avery. I think I have since the night I met you."

My heart stumbles and I grip him closer to me. "You what?"

"You want to hear it again?" he says, his mouth teasing my ear. "Greedy."

"It wouldn't hurt," I admit.

His smile strikes me in all the soft, tender places inside me. "You tell me first and I will."

"You've already said it!" He slides deep and I groan. "Okay. You're right. I love you, too. I think that's why I ran the first time. You scared the shit out of me." Then he kisses me hard and when I have a moment to breathe, I gasp. "We'll talk later."

And then he smiles and it's blinding, and I realize we'll have forever now for I love yous. For our family. For us.

Forever with him sounds like the best sort of beginning I could imagine.

Like a rainbow after a hurricane.

EPILOGUE

WALKER

Gracie toddles along the beach, dark hair flying behind her. Avery had tried to tame it into pigtails, but the girl wasn't having any of it. She gets her stubbornness from her mother and her fire from me.

The salty sea air carries Gracie's pleased shouts to me several lengths behind them. When she glances back to look for me, then dashes off—content to find that I'm still there, I know I made the right decision, staying. I never would have forgiven myself for leaving her.

Or Avery.

"Are you gonna help?" Avery asks with an amused glance back at me. Like our daughter, she checks to see that I'm still there. She's always pleased to find that I haven't gone anywhere. I don't mind. Avery hasn't had a lot of people she can depend on. I get it now, having gotten to know her for more than a night together. She's always had to rely on herself and she may not have made the best decision, but she did what she thought was right. I can't fault her for that. I can't say what I would have done in her situation. Scared. Pregnant. Alone. The weight of the world on her shoulders.

"You seem to have it under control," I say. And she does, but she knows I'm always there, if not by her side then right behind her. She's never had anyone else to depend on, but she can depend on me. And I'll spend every last breath making sure she knows it.

"Fine, but you get naps today," come her sassy response, then she's off chasing after the little girl in a highlighter pink bathing suit.

Mexico Beach isn't what it used to be. The coast had been wiped clean after Hurricane Michael. Homes, business, places the 850 made memories completely erased. The El Governor Motel, where I'd stayed a thousand times, was a husk of it's former self. There aren't many tourists now because there simply isn't much to see. Swaths of beach bordered by wreckage. Maybe that's why I like to take my girls here. Because it may not be pretty, but it's home. Like Battleboro has always been home.

Our little town may have been hit hard, but it's still standing, it's people rebuilding stronger than ever. Sure, it's not the 24/7 action I'm used to seeing as a Wildland Firefighter, but it suits me now, strangely. One of the guys at work, a real pain in the ass named Remington "Remy" Davis says it's because I'm getting old and need to settle down. Hell, maybe he's not wrong. Though his ass isn't anywhere near settling down and he's got a couple years on me.

Hell, maybe he's right.

Of the small team at Battleboro Fire & Rescue, I was somewhat of an outsider. Remy and the other guys on my shift, Alec Dorran, Jackson "Jax" Grady, and our Captain, Ezekiel "Zeke" Ross, are lifers. They've been on a team for going on a decade. Even though I was the outsider, they didn't really treat me like one. When I signed on to replace Tom Barry, who'd been killed during the storm, they welcomed me with open arms and a cold one.

Life couldn't get any better.

Avery finally manages to catch up to Gracie and I smile as they tumble into the surf, giggling until they can barely breath. Their heads dip close together and they come up with identical mischievous grins. I think to myself the same thing I thought when I first saw Avery. *I'm in trouble.*

They break into a run and tackle me. I let them take me down into the white sand, not caring that water soaks into my collar and my shorts fill with damp sand.

"Gotcha, Daddy!" Gracie says through wild laughter. "We gotchu."

I roll nimbly to my knees, picking Gracie up and tossing her into the air. She squeals and wiggles until I do it again. "Looks like I gotchu this time, Gracie-girl."

I throw her until my arms go numb.

"'Gain, 'gain," she begs.

"Sorry, baby, Daddy is worn slap out. Why don't we find somewhere for lunch and a beer?" I suggest.

"Beer!" she parrots gleefully.

I shrug away Avery's exasperated smile. "You can have one, too," I say to placate her.

"Where should we go?" I ask Gracie as I tote her the long walk back to the car.

"Pizza!" she shouts so loud it makes my ears ring.

"Of course," Avery says. "Pizza does sound great. I"m starving."

"Pizza it is." Whatever my girls want.

Crazy Beach Pizza is a short drive from the beach and we

fall on slices oozing with grease and cheese like we haven't eaten in a week. I wash mine down with a cold beer, then wait as the girls go for seconds.

My fingers play idly with the tip of Avery's ponytail as she carefully cuts Gracie's pizza into little bites. Man, I could get used to this. Two years later and I haven't. I hope it always feels brand new. I hope there's always a surprise, another adventure around the corner.

"What is it?" Avery asks.

"Nothing. Just…happy."

"You mean you're glad you got a beer," she teases.

I kiss the smile off her face, until her eyes go dark with lust and her pizza drops to her plate. "It means I'm glad I've got you."

"Me, too, me, too!" Gracie says until I give her a smacking kiss.

"I'm glad I've got you, too," I tell her.

Continue the Battleboro Fire & Rescue Series with…
Shielding His Heart!

ACKNOWLEDGMENTS

To the girl who spent her childhood buried in books, thank you for never giving up. For following your dreams.

To my mom, the best mother in the whole world. You're always there when I need you, no matter what. I love you to the moon and back.

Afton and Charlotte, I hope you're not reading this HAHA. I appreciate you for inspiring me to always do better, work harder. I wouldn't be where I am if it weren't for you both.

To Charlie. Always! Life with you is better than books.

A huge thank you to the girls in Nicole's Knockouts for motivating me each day to keep working and writing. I can't tell you how much it means to me to have you in my corner.

To the team who bring a book from production to publication including, but not limited to, IndieSage PR, editor Emily A. Lawrence, and the countless book bloggers and bookstagrammers THANK YOU!

ABOUT NICOLE BLANCHARD

Nicole Blanchard is the *New York Times* and *USA Today* best-selling author of dangerous romance from antiheroes to aliens. She and her family reside in the south along with menagerie of animals. Visit her website www.authornicoleblan chard.com for signed paperbacks, free books, and more!

ALSO BY NICOLE BLANCHARD

Battleboro Fire & Rescue Series

Storming His Heart

Shielding His Heart

Saving His Heart

First to Fight Series

Anchor

Warrior

Valor

Box Set: Books 1-3

Survivor

Savior

Honor

Box Set: Books 4-6

Traitor

Operator

Aviator

Captor

Protector

Armor

Friend Zone Series

Friend Zone

Frenemies

Friends with Benefits

Box Set

The Lost Planet Series

The Forgotten Commander

The Vanished Specialist

The Mad Lieutenant

Journey to the Lost Planet (Books 1-3)

The Uncertain Scientist

The Lonely Orphan

The Rogue Captain

Return to the Lost Planet (Books 4-6)

The Determined Hero

The Arrogant Genius

The Runaway Alien

Saving the Lost Planet (Books 7-9)

Dark Romance

Toxic

An Immortal Fairy Tale Series

Deal with the Dragon

Standalone Novellas

Bear with Me

Darkest Desires

Mechanical Hearts

www.ingramcontent.com/pod-product-compliance
Lightning Source LLC
Chambersburg PA
CBHW060506300726
48975CB00008B/2668